Grandpa Never Lies

by Ralph Fletcher

illustrated by Harvey Stevenson

Clarion Books • New York

Clarion Books
a Houghton Mifflin Company imprint
215 Park Avenue South, New York, NY 10003
Text copyright © 2000 by Ralph Fletcher
Illustrations copyright © 2000 by Harvey Stevenson

The illustrations were executed in acrylic paint.
The text was set in 17–point Hadriano Bold.

Printed in Hong Kong.

Library of Congress Cataloging-in-Publication Data

Fletcher, Ralph J.
Grandpa never lies / by Ralph Fletcher ; illustrated by Harvey Stevenson.
p.   cm.
Summary: A poetic description of the special relationship
between a grandfather and a young child.
ISBN 0-395-79770-5
1. Grandfathers—Juvenile poetry. 2. Children's poetry, American.
[1. Grandfathers—Poetry. 2. American poetry.] I. Stevenson, Harvey, ill. II. Title.
PS3556. L523G72 2000
811'.54–dc21   98-47020
CIP
AC

SPC 10 9 8 7 6 5 4 3 2 1

for Marian Reiner,
who nurtures my poems and stories
when they are tiny flames
—R.F.

*S*ummers are the best.
I get to spend a whole month at
Grandma and Grandpa's little
house in the woods.

We eat Grandma's blueberry pancakes,
track wild deer,
hunt trilobite fossils,
swim, play cards,
but mostly just talk.

When I ask what happened to Grandpa's hair,
he tells me, "A roaring tornado made me bald—
blew off my hair as it twisted through."

And Grandpa never lies,
so I know it's true.

When I visit on cold fall days,
we drink hot chocolate while Grandpa
reads from a book of fairy tales.

I see on the windows the blooming frost
and ask about those delicate lines.

Grandpa tells me about the winter elves
who come at dusk with magical brushes
to sketch on glass their silvery hues.

And Grandpa never lies,
so I know it's true.

In winter Grandpa and I go on long walks.

We always stop at Tolliver's barn
to pull down wicked icicle swords,
each one filled with sharp, clear light,
and challenge each other to a sword fight.

Grandpa tells me
how the wind works at night,
sharpening icicles as they grow.

And Grandpa never lies,
so I know it's so.

Then Grandma died.
Suddenly.
At the funeral I was too shocked to cry.

A month later Grandpa took me ice fishing at night.

He held my hand while we crossed Spy Pond
and showed me how to cut out circles of ice.

When I asked if he missed Grandma,
fat young tears rolled down his cheeks.
We could hear the ice settle and moan.

He said, "Ice this deep can talk to you."

And Grandpa never lies, so I know it's true.

It's spring now.
Grandpa's visiting.

We like to wake up, just he and I,
and sneak outside at sunrise while
diamonds dance all over the lawn.

He explains to me how spiders work,
stringing water beads on the finest thread,
decorating their webs with morning dew.

And Grandpa never lies,
so I know it's true.

Mornings we eat cereal on the porch
and make plans for the summer,
when I'll get to spend a whole month
at Grandpa's little house in the woods.

We'll dig for crystals,
sleep under the stars,
swim, play cards,
but mostly just talk.

When he asks,
"What's your favorite thing?"
I tell him, "Spending time with you."

And I never lie, so Grandpa knows it's true.